BUT I WANTED A BABY
BROTHER!

Kate Feiffer

ILLUSTRATED BY Diane Goode

A PAULA WISEMAN BOOK

Simon & Schuster Books for Young Readers · New York London Toronto Sydney

To Jonas and Drew
—K. F.

For Peter ♥
—D. G.

SIMON & SCHUSTER BOOKS FOR YOUNG READERS · An imprint of Simon & Schuster Children's Publishing Division · 1230 Avenue of the Americas, New York, New York 10020 · Text copyright © 2010 by Kate Feiffer · Illustrations copyright © 2010 by Diane Goode · All rights reserved, including the right of reproduction in whole or in part in any form. · SIMON & SCHUSTER BOOKS FOR YOUNG READERS is a trademark of Simon & Schuster, Inc. · For information about special discounts for bulk purchases, please contact Simon & Schuster Special Sales at 1-866-506-1949 or business@simonandschuster.com. · The Simon & Schuster Speakers Bureau can bring authors to your live event. For more information or to book an event, contact the Simon & Schuster Speakers Bureau at 1-866-248-3049 or visit our website at www.simonspeakers.com. · Book design by Jessica Handelman · The text for this book is set in Fairfield LH. · The illustrations for this book are rendered in watercolor. · Manufactured in China · 0510 SCP · 10 9 8 7 6 5 4 3 · Library of Congress Cataloging-in-Publication Data · Feiffer, Kate. · But I wanted a baby brother! / by Kate Feiffer ; illustrated by Diane Goode. — 1st ed. · p. cm. · "A Paula Wiseman Book." · Summary: Oliver Keaton wants a baby brother more than anything but when he gets a baby sister instead, he sets out with his dog Chaplin to trade his sister for the perfect baby brother. · ISBN 978-1-4169-3941-2 (hardcover : alk. paper) · [1. Brother and sisters—Fiction. 2. Family life—Fiction. 3. Humorous stories.] I. Goode, Diane, ill. II. Title. · PZ7.F33346Bu 2010 · [E]—dc22 · 2009033320

Autobiography of
OLIVER KEATON
by Oliver Keaton

My name is Oliver Keaton. My initials are O. K.
I have one dog. His name is Chaplin. I don't have
any sisters and I don't want a sister. I want a
brother. I've wanted a brother for my entire life.
My favorite thing to do is ride my bike. I like playing
baseball. I know a big secret. No one told me,
but I figured it out by looking at my mom.
I'm getting a baby brother. I can't wait.

OLIVER KEATON wanted a baby brother more than anything and he thought he was about to get exactly what he wanted. But on the morning of Tuesday, February 2nd, Oliver got a baby sister . . .

. . . by mistake.

No one else seemed to notice the mistake.

In fact, everyone looked very happy, as if there had been no mistake at all.

His parents grinned and guffawed. His grandparents chuckled and cheered. His neighbors brought presents, but not for Oliver . . .

. . . or for Chaplin, who didn't look
happy either. He probably wanted
a brother too.

Oliver tried looking happy.
He tried very hard.

He tried in the morning, when he asked his mom,

And he tried at night, when he asked his dad,

But he couldn't look happy, no matter how hard he tried, when his parents said, "Isn't your sister adorable?" instead of "Yes, Oliver, you'll have a baby brother in a few weeks."

And it was impossible to look happy when they said, "She looks just like you, Oliver." Because if she really looked just like him, SHE'D BE A HE!!!!

Had everyone except for Chaplin forgotten that Oliver wanted a brother?

At least his sister's name was Julie, so he could secretly call her Julian. And she was bald. Not many girls are bald.

If he thought really hard, he could think of some things she did as well as his baby brother would have done, if he had a baby brother, which he DIDN'T!

She gurgled . . .

kicked . . .

smiled . . .

and slept . . .

. . . like a baby brother.

But sometimes she wore dresses and that was bad.

And she never threw the ball back. A baby brother would have known how to throw a ball.

Hopefully he'd get a baby brother soon.

Because if he wasn't going to get a baby brother, he'd have to . . .

. . . replace Julie.

Oliver told Chaplin, "Any baby will do. I'm not picky as long as it's a boy."

Then Oliver's best friend, Tom, got a new baby brother. Tom already had two brothers. Oliver figured he didn't need another one.

He invited Tom over for a playdate and asked, "Do you want to trade?"

Tom carefully examined Julie.

Oliver and Chaplin decided Tom's baby
brother wouldn't work out after all.

Oliver and Chaplin remembered that a girl in his class had a new baby brother. Mary probably wanted a baby sister. Right?

Julie already knew how to sleep through the night. She was smart for a baby sister.

That night Oliver and Chaplin decided that if they got a baby brother, he had to be smarter than Julie. Julie knew how to wave. She never pulled Chaplin's fur, and she could crawl really fast.

On Saturday Oliver and Chaplin went to look for a smart baby in the park.

The park was filled with smart babies. Even Oliver's parents said the babies looked smart.

But the baby that Oliver thought looked the smartest was a . . .

. . . girl. She had a huge pink ribbon stuck in her hair. Julie never wore pink ribbons in her hair.

She didn't even have hair.

Oliver asked his parents if they could go to the zoo.

They saw boy babies looking at tigers and boy babies laughing at seals. They saw sleepy, happy, and angry boy babies. None of them looked as fun as Julie.

For some unknown reason, at that moment of pondering, Oliver looked up. High above his head he saw a sign.

Under the sign he saw a door.

Crying babies went in through the door. Happy babies came out. Girl babies went in. Boy babies came out.

"This is where you go to change your girl baby for a boy baby," said Oliver. "Come on, Chaplin, let's look for a brother." With heads and tail held high, they marched in . . .

Yuck!

. . . and ran back out
very, very quickly!

Oliver and Chaplin kept looking for a baby brother.
They looked up streets on the way to school and
down streets on the way home.

They buzzed past barbershops . . .

. . . and checked the classified ads, just in case someone was selling a used baby boy.

After ten months and two days, they had examined one hundred
and six baby boys.

They saw baby boys with curly hair, straight hair, long hair,
and no hair, just like Julie.

Some looked like good baby brothers—but for other boys,
not Oliver.

So they searched some more.

One year and seventeen hours after they started looking, there was nowhere else to look.

They did the only thing left to do.

They gave up.

Julie crawled faster, laughed louder, and was more fun to play with than any of the baby brothers out there. She had even learned to throw a ball.

Oliver, Julie, and Chaplin played together all
day long. They slept in the same room at night.

But when Oliver's father announced, "We're having another baby," it only took twelve seconds before Oliver decided that once again, he wanted a baby brother more than anything.

And sure enough, some endless
months later, Oliver got . . .

another baby sister.

The end?